A First-Start® Easy Reader

This easy reader contains only 41 different words,
repeated often to help the young reader develop
word recognition and interest in reading.

Basic word list for *Home for a Puppy*

a	have	one
and	home	please
black	homes	puppies
brown	how	puppy
can	I	see
Daisy	keep	tan
Daisy's	know	the
each	let's	this
find	me	three
for	must	to
four	need	two
free	needs	we
good	now	will
has		with

Home for a Puppy

Written by Sharon Gordon

Illustrated by Jody Wheeler

Troll Associates

Library of Congress Cataloging in Publication Data

Gordon, Sharon.
    Home for a puppy.

    Summary: In this easy-to-read story, a young boy
finds homes for four puppies.
    [1. Dogs—Fiction]   I. Wheeler, Jody, ill.
II. Title.
PZ7.G65936Ho   1987   [E]   86-30853
ISBN 0-8167-0978-5 (lib. bdg.)
ISBN 0-8167-0979-3 (pbk.)

Daisy has four puppies.

Daisy has a black puppy . . .
a brown puppy . . .

a tan puppy . . .

and a black and brown
and tan puppy!

We must find homes
for Daisy's puppies.

We must find a good home
for each puppy.

We will need four homes . . .
for four puppies.

"I know how to find homes
for the puppies!"

"I will find four good homes for Daisy's puppies."

"Puppies For Free.

Four Free Puppies!"

"Let's see the puppies."

"Can we keep the black puppy, please?"

Now we need three homes . . .
for three puppies.

"Puppies For Free.
Three Free Puppies!"

"Let's see the puppies."

"Can we keep the brown puppy, please?"

Now we need two homes . . .
for two puppies.

"Puppies For Free.
Two Free Puppies!"

"Let's see the puppies."

"Can we keep the tan puppy,
please?"

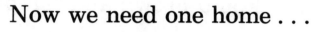

Now we need one home . . .
for one puppy.

A black and brown and tan puppy.

We must find a good home
for this puppy.

"I know a good home
for this puppy."

"*We* can keep the black and brown and tan puppy!"

"Can we please?"

"This puppy needs a good home."

"This puppy will have a good home with Daisy and me!"